P9-DWO-063

CALGARY PUBLIC LIBRARY

DEC   2016

**CUENTO
DE LUZ**

*To Ariel,
my love, my companion, and the best father in the world.
May we inspire each other every day, so that the most beautiful thing within us grows and grows.*

The Magic Hat Shop

Text & illustrations © 2016 Sonja Wimmer
This edition © 2016 Cuento de Luz SL
Calle Claveles, 10 | Urb. Monteclaro | Pozuelo de Alarcón | 28223 | Madrid | Spain
www.cuentodeluz.com
Title in Spanish: La sombrería mágica
English translation by Jon Brokenbrow

ISBN: 978-84-16147-19-9

Printed by Shanghai Chenxi Printing Co., Ltd. January 2016, print number 1546-2

All rights reserved

FSC
www.fsc.org
MIX
Paper from
responsible sources
FSC® C007923

The MAGIC HAT SHOP

Sonja Wimmer

Nobody knew how it arrived, or from where, but one morning a little hat shop just appeared, right in the middle of the town square.

"Who needs hats?" said some of the townspeople, while others said, "How rude, turning up just like that!"

They looked at the shop out of the corner of their eyes and kept away, mistrusting anything that might threaten the quiet routine of the town.

The first person who dared to enter the shop was a young man called Timid Tim. He was so shy he never spoke to anyone, and he always seemed to be making great efforts to go unnoticed.

But when he walked out the door, just a few moments later, he was wearing a wonderful hat on his head. And not only that: something else about him had changed.

Before, he'd always walked around with his shoulders hunched up, looking down at the ground. Now he seemed to have grown a couple of inches. He was walking with his back straight, his chin held high, and he even said "Hello!" to the people in the square, who looked at him in surprise.

Little by little, the townspeople
plucked up the courage to enter
the store. At first it was just out of
curiosity, making sure nobody else
was watching. But when they came
out, they were all wearing new hats,
and they seemed to have been
changed in some wonderful way.

People started to whisper that the hats
were magic, because they brought
out the most surprising features in the
people who wore them, and made all
of their problems vanish into thin air.

Sad Sally had almost forgotten how to smile, from lack of practice. But from the moment she put on her new hat, she began to greet each new day with laughter, spreading happiness to everyone around her.

Mean Morris had a new top hat.
Before, he'd never spared a thought
for anyone else, but now he always
left the door of his house open.

Anyone who felt like dropping by
was invited to have a cup of tea, to
share their problems, or just to sit a
while and chat.

People said that the hatter
never spoke a single word,
but he knew how to listen
carefully to his customers,
until he found the hat that
was just right for them.

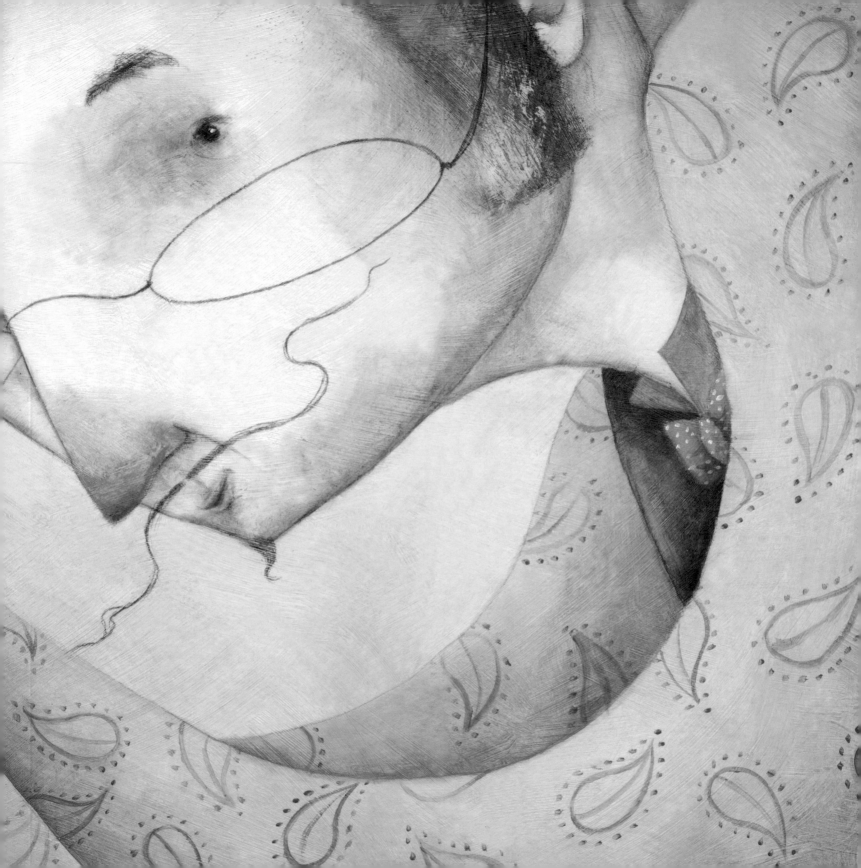

The mayor, who thought he was the grandest of all the town's inhabitants by far, called himself the Great Grazinski.

One morning, after chatting to the hatter about all the wonderful things he'd done, the Great Grazinski asked: "So, do you have a hat worthy of a celebrity such as myself?"

The hatter, who had been listening carefully, just like he did with all of his customers, winked and nodded his head.

Shortly afterwards, the Great Grazinski strode out of the store with a huge smile on his face. Suddenly he didn't feel quite as grand as he used to; he felt different, and very happy with his new hat.

Life in the town had certainly changed since the silent, mysterious hatter had arrived with his magic store.

The townspeople didn't want to take off their hats. They wore them in the street, at home, when they ate, and when they kissed. They didn't take them off when they went to bed, or when they had a shower.

But one day, a terrible storm swept through the town. A ferocious wind blew all the leaves off the trees, and all the hats off of everyone's heads. They flew away into the air, and were never seen again.

The following morning, once the storm had
passed, the townspeople realized that the
wind had not only swept away all of their
hats, but it had also taken the little store.
The only thing that was left of the hatter
was his derby.

Silence fell over the townspeople like a thick
fog. What would become of them now? They
felt bare and weak without their hats.

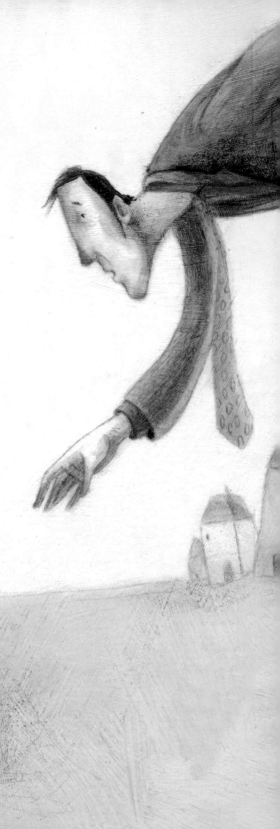

"I don't want to be shy ever again!" said Tim, all of a sudden. "We don't need magic hats to become the people we really want to be!"

"You're so brave! You'd be a much better mayor than me!" said the Great Grazinski, in a soft voice.

Mean Morris added, "And if we help each other, I'm sure we can do it!"

Sad Sally, who wasn't sad any more, put her arm around Timid Tim, who wasn't shy any more, and began to dance with him. Soon all of the townspeople were singing and dancing through the streets.

As for the hatter, nobody ever heard from him again. Some said that the wind had carried him away, along with his little store.

Others said that he'd disappeared inside his derby, and would reappear somewhere else where he could start selling his magical hats all over again.